For my very own Big Bear and Little Fish —S.N.

To my mom and dad —I.S.N.

Carolrhoda Books®
An imprint of Lerner Publishing Group, Inc.
241 First Avenue North
Minneapolis, MN 55401 USA

For reading levels and more information, look up this title at www.lernerbooks.com.

Designed by Emily Harris.
Main body text set in Mikado. Typeface provided by HVD Fonts.
The illustrations in this book were created with Adobe Fresco.

Library of Congress Cataloging-in-Publication Data

Names: Nickel, Sandra, author. | Na, Il Sung, illustrator.
Title: Big Bear and little Fish / Sandra Nickel ; illustrated by Il Sung Na.
Description: Minneapolis : Carolrhoda Books, [2022] | Audience: Ages 4-8. | Audience: Grades K-1. | Summary: Despite their many differences, Big Bear and a Little Fish find similarities between themselves and become friends.
Identifiers: LCCN 2021051133 (print) | LCCN 2021051134 (ebook) | ISBN 9781728417172 (library binding) | ISBN 9781728460529 (ebook) | ISBN 9781728460567 (ebook)
Subjects: CYAC: Friendship—Fiction. | Bears—Fiction. | Fishes—Fiction. | LCGFT: Picture books.
Classification: LCC PZ7.1.N5335 Bi 2022 (print) | LCC PZ7.1.N5335 (ebook) | DDC [E]—dc23

LC record available at https://lccn.loc.gov/2021051133
LC ebook record available at https://lccn.loc.gov/2021051134

Manufactured in the United States of America
1-48971-49231-12/7/2021

BIG BEAR
AND LITTLE FiSH

Sandra Nickel

illustrated by Il Sung Na

Carolrhoda Books
Minneapolis

Bear wanted a teddy bear.

Not just any teddy bear.

She wanted the biggest one of all.

Bear got a fish instead.

It was small. It was very small.

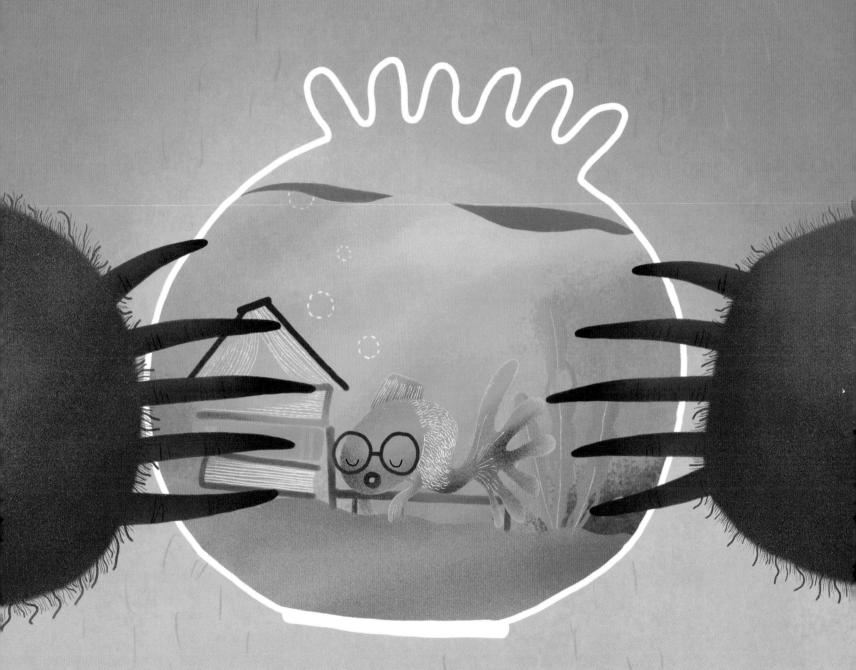

It was so small it lived in a bowl.

The fish woke up and smiled. "Hello, Bear.
Is this my new home?"

Bear was big. She was very big. She was
so big she worried she might scare Fish
with her big, booming voice.

Bear did not say, "Hello."

Instead, because it was lunchtime,
Bear went inside and made a sandwich.
She was gold and liked golden food,
especially bread and syrup.

Bear did not make lunch for Fish.
Fish was orange and probably ate
carrot muffins and cheese.

Or tangerines and pumpkins.

Bear didn't have any of those things.

If only Fish were a teddy bear.

Bear pulled out her yardstick for
her after-lunch measuring.

She sized herself up from the tops of her ears to the tips of her toes.

She was nine feet and eight inches big!

Bear did not size up Fish. She wasn't sure where to begin. Did you go side to side? Or top to bottom? And where exactly was a fish's bottom, anyway?

Bear tried to figure it out, but before she could decide, it was time for her afternoon walk. If only Fish were a teddy bear.

Bear blew some fluff in the air. She balanced a leaf
on her nose. She admired a bush.

Bear was pretty sure Fish did not take walks. Fluff would land in her water. Or a leaf would get caught in her tail.

If Fish were a teddy bear, Bear wouldn't have to think about any of that. They would just amble and ramble, and never once fuss about tails.

Bear ambled up a hill and down again. It was a very, very big walk. And all the while, Bear worried that she should never have brought Fish home.

At last, Bear turned around and headed back.

Fish was exactly where Bear had left her. "Hello, Bear. How was your walk? I have to say, this porch of ours is splendid."

"I am sorry, Fish, but you cannot stay."

"Why not?" asked Fish.

"You are orange. You eat carrot muffins and tangerines."

"I do like muffins. But aren't you orange too?"

Bear peeked at her stomach. It was an orangey sort of gold. It looked an awful lot like a carrot muffin.

"I am sorry, Fish. You still cannot stay. You have a tail. A leaf might get caught in it when we go for walks."

"Hmm," said Fish.
"Don't you have a tail?
There, behind you."

Bear twisted around. She discovered a
bit of fur. It looked very much like a tail.

"I am sorry, Fish. You still cannot stay. Most of all, it is because you are small."

"Am I? I always wanted to be measured."

Bear brought her yardstick. Fish lined herself up from the end of her nose to the tip of her tail. She was three inches long.

"That is not so small," said Fish. "I am not one inch. I am not two inches. I am three inches."

"Three inches is very small. You are so small you live in a bowl!"

"But don't you live in a bowl too?"

Bear looked around. The sky was as round as Fish's bowl, only upside down.

She looked and looked at her round blue bowl.

At last, Bear said, "I think I might be small."

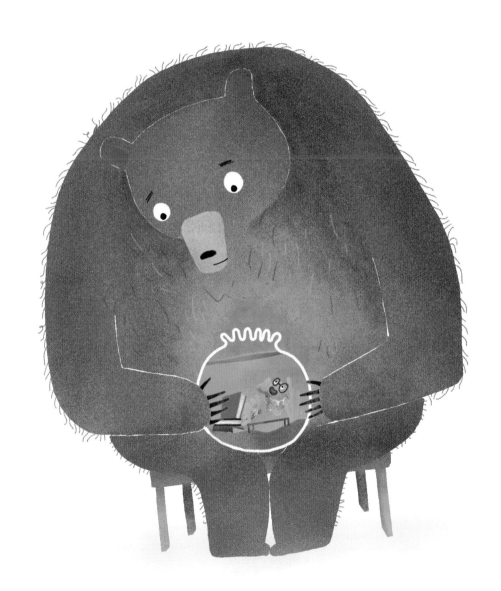

"Everybody is sometimes," said Fish.

"But don't worry, Bear. No matter how small we might be on the outside, we can still be big on the inside."

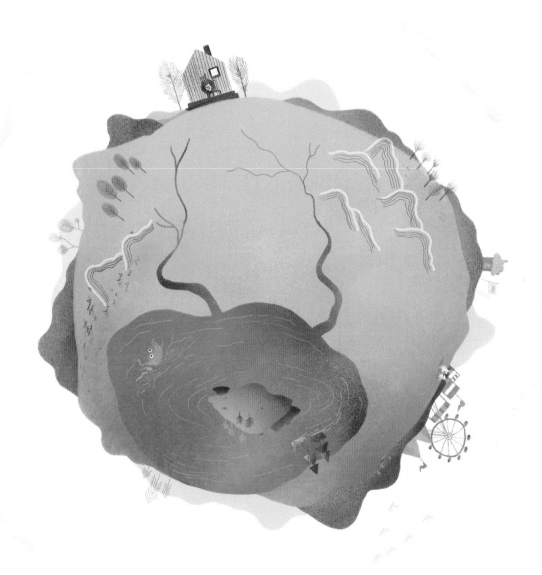

"Oh," said Bear. "I never thought of that."

"Hmm," said Bear.

"Yes?" asked Fish.

"I think I would like to amble a bit more—this time with you. We might even find a carrot muffin."

"I would like that," said Fish.
"Especially if it's a very big muffin."

And so they ambled and
rambled. And never once
fussed about tails.